Samuel Drew Hasn't a Clue

Gabby Dawnay & Alex Barrow

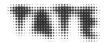

The day is fine - the sky is bright
As Samuel Drew strolls into sight.
He pulls behind a splendid thing,
A giant parcel tied with string!

The package wobbles, stuck with tape,
A lovely box so square of shape,
Wrapped-up in coloured tissue paper.
Off they roll at quite a caper.

A pigeon spies it from a tree,
"Hey, what's in there? Do let me see!"

The paper package bumps and shakes,
The pigeon cries, "Could it be . . . cakes . . . ?"

"A box like that – it *must* be treats!"
Another nearby pigeon tweets.
"Banana bread and butterscotch . . ."

By now the other pigeons watch.
"A spongy bake - a birthday cake?
Oh let us peep, for goodness sake!"

"A cake with icing, cream and jam!
Or croissants filled with cheese and ham!"

"What's in your parcel, Samuel Drew?
We need to know! Give us a clue!"

"Did someone mention ham?" says fox,
"Have you got ham inside your box?"

"It smells of . . . hmm, my favourite treat!
I think it could be . . . yes, it's meat!"

"A leg of lamb, a juicy steak,
So big it gives me tummy ache!
Unless my nose is much mistaken,
I can smell a bit of bacon."

"What's in your parcel, Samuel Drew?
We need to know! Give us a clue!"

A dog appears and with a whoop,
He joins the rather greedy group.
"I smell it too! It's chicken stew!
With bags of bones to crunch and chew,"

"Or pizza with tomato sauce?
And mozzarella cheese, of course."

"A tasty pie, all hot and savoury,
Filled with carrots, meat and gravy!"
"A pie? A pie!" the pigeons cry,
"Share it! Share it! Don't be shy!"

"What's in your parcel Samuel Drew?
We need to know! Give us a clue!"

"But maybe it's another dish?
I think I smell a hint of . . . fish?"
"Did someone mention fish?" says cat,
"You see I'm very fond of that!"

"Salmon cakes or cod fish fingers,
Fish - the smell that always lingers!
Fish for breakfast, lunch and tea.
Please say your gift is fish for meeeee(ouw)!"

Cat licks her lips and then her paws,
"I think a box as big as yours
Must surely hide a dish or two . . ."

"What's in your parcel Samuel Drew?
WE NEED TO KNOW! GIVE US A CLUE!"

Pizza? Roast? Sardines on toast?
What is the snack YOU like the most?

"A snack? A snack!" the ducks all quack.
(They look as if they might attack)

The squirrels ask without a fuss,
"Do you have any nuts for us?"

A rat appears and flicks his tail,
Then quickly joins the busy trail,
"What's in your parcel tied with string?
I don't care – I'll eat anything!"

The pigeons start to flap and prance,
The cat and fox exchange a glance,
"We'd settle for a pigeon pie . . ."
The pigeons gulp! And off they fly.

Be it cakes or fish or stew,
We need to know, we really do!
And don't YOU want to know it, too?
WHAT'S IN YOUR PARCEL, SAMUEL DREW?!

Sam looks around, "I wish I knew . . .
I haven't got the faintest clue!"

"But I must run because, you see,
My birthday party starts at three
And if you really want to know,
You're all invited – come, let's go!"

And back at Sam's there is a feast
For every bird and every beast!
But what's inside that lovely box?
A bat? A ball? A pair of socks?

You must have noticed all the clues
Along the streets and in the news?
Do look, the final page reveals
Sam's favourite toy - a . . .

dog-on-wheels!

Also available . . .

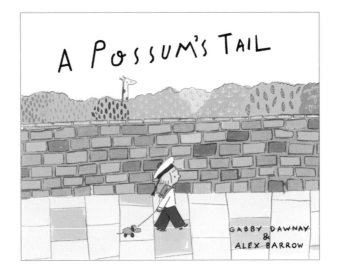

For Bumpy G.D.

For Tita Maggie A.B.

First published 2019 by order of the Tate Trustees by Tate Publishing,
a division of Tate Enterprises Ltd, Millbank, London SW1P 4RG
www.tate.org.uk/publishing

A catalogue record for this book is available from the British Library
ISBN 978-1-84976-642-5

Distributed in the United States and Canada by ABRAMS, New York
Library of Congress Control Number applied for
Colour reproduction by DL Imaging Ltd, London
Printed in China by Toppan Leefung Printing Ltd